COYOTE STORIES FOR CHILDREN
Tales from Native America

Adapted by
Susan Strauss

Illustrations by
Gary Lund

Beyond Words Publishing, Inc.

For Brave Buffalo, who welcomed me into the wisdom
of his cultural traditions . . . who, with humor and
patience, looked beyond how the dominant culture
had formed me, to my real yearning for the old
wisdoms and the sacred.

Beyond Words Publishing, Inc.
13950 NW Pumpkin Ridge Road
Hillsboro, OR 97123
(503) 647-5109

Printed by D.W. Friesen & Sons in Canada.

ISBN: 0-941831-61-2 (cloth)
ISBN: 0-941831-62-0 (paper)

Introduction

Just who is Coyote? This is a question that will keep giving answers with each Coyote tale we hear. If you mention Coyote's name among Native Americans, you will probably see smiles bloom across their faces. This Coyote is not the wild animal jumping about in the sagebrush landscapes of the American West, although he seems to have been somewhat inspired by his animal relative in the wild. The coyote has miraculously managed to survive widespread hunting, trapping, and poison-baiting since the late 1800s. Western ranchers and government predator-control programs have waged an all-out war designed to eliminate this perceived threat to livestock, and millions of coyotes have been killed. But throughout this war, coyotes have managed to wise up to hunting and trapping techniques, increase their population, and extend the range of places where they live.

Native people say that the Creator gave Coyote the power to come back to life after he died and the power to create whatever he could imagine. Old Man Coyote, as Native Americans call him, is both a mythic hero and a sacred fool. Stories of his adventures show how he created good things in the world with his powerful imagination and how he defeated monsters with his cleverness and resilience.

Unlike his wild cousin, the mythic Old Man Coyote is also very foolish. If the wild coyote were as foolish as the mythic Coyote, he would never have survived the past hundred years. In his foolishness,

Old Man Coyote acts more like human beings — especially the kind of human behavior that Native Americans consider particularly offensive. He can be arrogant, greedy, and self-centered. Native children — and people of all ages — love to listen to Coyote stories, because they get to delight in Coyote's "bad-boy" antics and learn about the consequences of such foolishness without having to make the same mistakes in their own lives. While laughing at Coyote with their friends and family, Native children learn how to behave and how not to behave. This is why Coyote is a sacred fool. This clown gives us a way to know and accept ourselves. His foolish mistakes and his heroic imagination teach about balance and respect — two of the most important values shared by all Native people. This is the balance in ourselves and in our inter-relationships with all life-forms. As a Pueblo man once told me, "Now I understand why my grandmother told me Coyote stories. She was teaching me about balance: the potential for creating good and bad that lives in each of us . . . that we must see this potential in ourselves and hold it in balance for things to go well in the world." At the begin-ning and at the end of the stories, Coyote is always traveling . . . making his tracks . . . tracks . . . tracks. He travels like this because this is the way the story shows us that he is everywhere and his spirit is in each of us.

"You just can't get rid of Old Man Coyote."

Agnes Vanderburg
Flathead Indian Elder

These Stories Are Sacred

A Modoc friend of mine told me, "Our stories are sacred. We only tell them at a special time of year. One story we only tell . . . when the winds are blowing across the lake. That way we can hear the spirits of the lake that the story speaks about."

What does it mean that stories are sacred? Does it mean that they should be withheld or received? Many traditional tellers only share their stories in the winter and at night. This is the best time for the listener to receive the story's wisdom. Stories need a special time to come out, because they speak truth in a different way than does the evening news.

Some people say, "Indians told stories to explain the world because they didn't have science." These people don't realize that a story contains many layers of truth. Native people hold their stories in silence from such a listener. If you heard a story or had a dream that touched you, would you share it with a person who would say, "Oh, that's just a fantasy"?

Black Elk, a very famous Sioux Medicine Man, was asked, "Are these stories true?" He answered, "Well, I don't know if they happened exactly that way, but if you listen to them long enough, you will hear how they are true." Maybe years from now you will remember a story which you once thought was ridiculous, and you will discover some-

thing wise in it, something that you didn't see before. Dreams and myths work in this way. They reveal their truth slowly over time. If I share a story with you, take care of what you make of this new story and how you share it.

I have gathered the stories in this collection from original recordings made in the last part of the nineteenth century. Some of them have been separated from their original landscape and a living storyteller for almost a hundred years. I let them speak to me about their landscape and the animal people who bring wisdom and humor alive in them. I added ways of speaking and thinking that I gathered from my Native friends and teachers. I share them with you in the hope that perhaps you will find a new piece of wisdom in them which I missed. Hold or share them with love and respect. They are the earliest stories to be born out of our homeland, this North American continent.

Susan Strauss
Bend, Oregon
September 1991

"You should always be in bare feet to tell these stories, because
the stories live in the earth . . . and they speak to us through our feet."
Ed Edmo, Sr.
Shoshone-Bannock elder

Coyote Gets His Powers
Okanogan (Great Basin)

Now, long ago . . . and I mean LONG ago . . . in the days before the coming of the human beings . . . there were only animal people. There were the four-leggeds . . . the deer people, the raccoon people, and the great big bear people. There were the snake people, the frog people, and the insect people. In those days there were even plant people and rock people. The rock people are the oldest people in the world. They were here before anyone else . . . and for that, they deserve a lot of respect.

Now . . . in those days . . . there came a great voice, and it spoke to all of the animal people:

"Some of you have names now. Some of you will need new names for when the human beings come. Come to my lodge in the morning and I will give you your new names."

This was the voice of the spirit . . . the spirit, Native people would say, that shoots up . . . and out . . . in all green things . . . the Creator.

Now . . . Coyote heard this! He was so excited about getting a new name that he went right out . . . walking all around the villages . . . BRAGGING to everyone about how he was going to get a new name. This is how Coyote spoke:

"I . . . Coyote . . . will be the first one to the Creator's lodge . . . Yeah! Then all of you will be calling me . . . aah . . . aah . . . Grizzly Bear! Yeah! Grizzly Bear, chief of the mountain people!"

And Coyote went on his way to the next village.

"Hey! I . . . Coyote . . . will stay up all night long . . . Yeah! I will be the first one to the Creator's lodge in the morning, and then all of you . . . will be calling me . . . aah . . . aah . . . Salmon! Yeah! Salmon, chief of the fish people!"

Coyote was always forgetting something, and if one of the animal people reminded him that he wanted the name Grizzly Bear, he'd say, "Oh, yeah! I knew that. I just forgot." Coyote went on his way from village to village bragging in this way.

Now . . . do you think that the animal people were listening to Coyote when he was bragging like this?

No, no, no. They knew about Coyote. Just like Native people know that there's going be trouble when someone starts thinking too much of themself. Oh yes, the animal people . . . they knew about Coyote. They knew about Coyote from the time when he was fooling around and shot the night. It seemed to be night forever until Old Man Duck fixed it. They knew about Coyote from the time when he saw Hummingbird Woman flying around. Well . . . you know how a Hummingbird can fly . . . don't you? *Pthip!* (up) *Pthip!* (down) *Pthip! Pthip!* (side to side) Coyote saw Hummingbird Woman flying like that, and he said that he could fly like that, too!

So, he climbed way up this tall ponderosa pine . . . to show everyone how well he could fly. He JUMPED OUT OF THAT TREE . . .

"Aaaaaaaaaah" . . .

SPLAT! Flat on the ground. Just like that!

So, ever since that time, the people gave him a special

name. Well, of course, his name was Coyote . . . but when he was acting like this, the people called him another name . . . They called him . . . "Senche-lay-ya! Senche-lay-ya!" It means braggart, fool, someone who thinks he is better than everyone else. Maybe you know someone who is a Senche-lay-ya.

Well, Coyote went on from village to village telling everyone . . . "Hey! I'm going to stay up all night long and then, for sure, I'll be the first one to the Creator's lodge. Then, all of you will be calling me . . ."

"Psst . . . psst!" It was Fox . . . Coyote's younger brother. "Hey, Coyote! You'd better be quiet. Everyone is calling you 'Senche-lay-ya' . . . Yip, yip, yip!"

"Aaah. . . let them call me 'Senche-lay-ya.' You will see, Fox. I am going to stay up all night long! Then, for sure, I will be the first one to the Creator's lodge . . . and even you, Fox . . . you're going to be calling me . . . aaah . . . aaah . . . Grizzly Bear! Yeah! Grizzly Bear, chief of the mountain people!"

Fox just sat there. His eyes were wide with disbelief. "I don't know, Coyote. I think you're going to have to keep your own name. . . Yip, yip, yip . . . Yeah!"

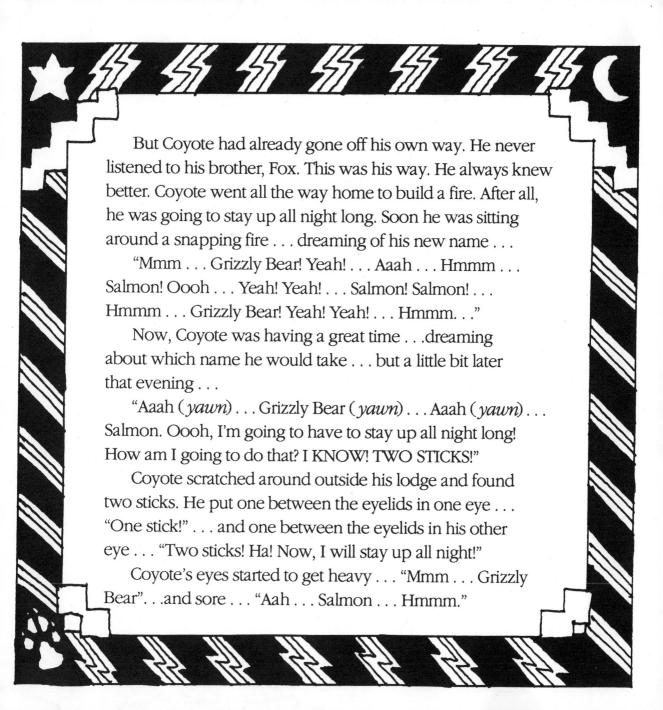

But Coyote had already gone off his own way. He never listened to his brother, Fox. This was his way. He always knew better. Coyote went all the way home to build a fire. After all, he was going to stay up all night long. Soon he was sitting around a snapping fire . . . dreaming of his new name . . .

"Mmm . . . Grizzly Bear! Yeah! . . . Aaah . . . Hmmm . . . Salmon! Oooh . . . Yeah! Yeah! . . . Salmon! Salmon! . . . Hmmm . . . Grizzly Bear! Yeah! Yeah! . . . Hmmm. . ."

Now, Coyote was having a great time . . .dreaming about which name he would take . . . but a little bit later that evening . . .

"Aaah (*yawn*) . . . Grizzly Bear (*yawn*) . . . Aaah (*yawn*) . . . Salmon. Oooh, I'm going to have to stay up all night long! How am I going to do that? I KNOW! TWO STICKS!"

Coyote scratched around outside his lodge and found two sticks. He put one between the eyelids in one eye . . . "One stick!" . . . and one between the eyelids in his other eye . . . "Two sticks! Ha! Now, I will stay up all night!"

Coyote's eyes started to get heavy . . . "Mmm . . . Grizzly Bear". . .and sore . . . "Aah . . . Salmon . . . Hmmm."

SNAP! "Nnnnnnn . . . zzzzzzzz."

Ooooh yes! Coyote did that! He fell right asleep. I bet you knew he was going to do that.

The next morning . . . when he woke up . . . he ran right out to the Creator's lodge. "Ah, I will take the name, Grizzly Bear. Yeah! Yip! Yip!"

"Grizzly Bear was taken at dawn."

"Well . . . aah . . . then, I will take the name, Salmon. Yeah! Yip! Yip!"

"Salmon swam away at dawn . . .   Noooooo . . . Coyote . . . You must keep your name. It is a good name for you. Soon the human beings, the two-leggeds, will be coming. You must make the world ready for them. To do this, I give you two powers. You have the power to CREATE WHATEVER YOU CAN IMAGINE . . . and you have the power to COME BACK TO LIFE AFTER YOU DIE . . . GOOOOOO OUT . . . COYOTE!"

Coyote felt so good about his powers that he forgot all about the other names. They didn't seem so important any-more. After all, he had his powers! He was going to create a

world with his imagination! In a way, you and I are a little like Coyote. We can create our world with the power of our imaginations, too. But, just like you and I, Coyote didn't always use his powers well. Sometimes he created beautiful and necessary things, and sometimes he created things out of his arrogance, self-centeredness, or impatience. Everything we two-leggeds must endure or get to enjoy in this world was created by Coyote. Coyote felt so good about his new powers that he set out traveling . . . making his tracks, tracks, tracks . . . traveling all over North America . . . making the world ready for the coming of the human people.

Monster Woman at the Coast
Wasco (Columbia Plateau)

Coyote was traveling across the Bitterroot Range of the Rocky Mountains. He made his tracks across the high desert of Eastern Oregon . . . tracks, tracks, tracks . . . he crossed over the Cascade Mountains . . . down through the lush Willamette Valley . . . over the Coast Range Mountains (you see, Coyote gets around!) . . . tracks, tracks, tracks . . . and down onto the sands of the wide-open Pacific Ocean.

There was a long line of animal people standing there . . . and staring out at the ocean.

Coyote came right up to the last person in line . . . "Hey, brother!" (You see, Coyote always speaks to other animals as relatives, because Native people respect all living beings as their relatives . . . believing that we are all related.)

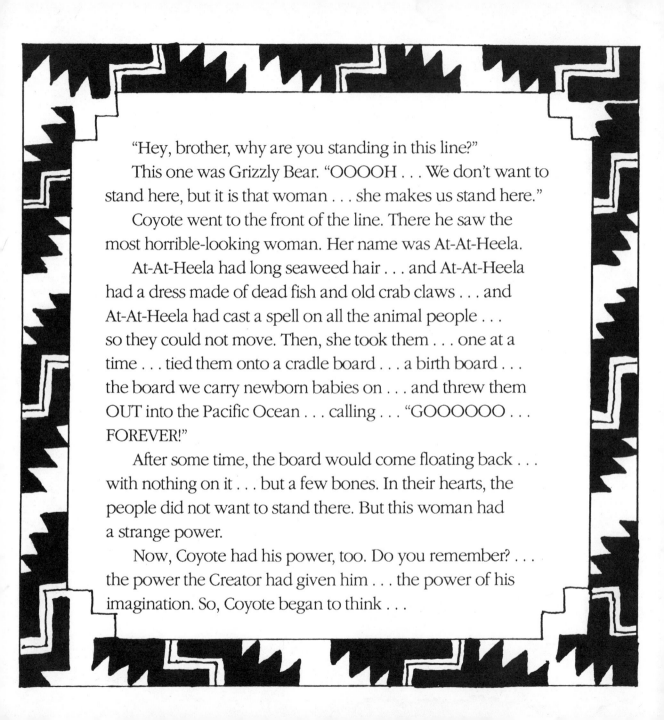

"Hey, brother, why are you standing in this line?"

This one was Grizzly Bear. "OOOOH . . . We don't want to stand here, but it is that woman . . . she makes us stand here."

Coyote went to the front of the line. There he saw the most horrible-looking woman. Her name was At-At-Heela.

At-At-Heela had long seaweed hair . . . and At-At-Heela had a dress made of dead fish and old crab claws . . . and At-At-Heela had cast a spell on all the animal people . . . so they could not move. Then, she took them . . . one at a time . . . tied them onto a cradle board . . . a birth board . . . the board we carry newborn babies on . . . and threw them OUT into the Pacific Ocean . . . calling . . . "GOOOOOO . . . FOREVER!"

After some time, the board would come floating back . . . with nothing on it . . . but a few bones. In their hearts, the people did not want to stand there. But this woman had a strange power.

Now, Coyote had his power, too. Do you remember? . . . the power the Creator had given him . . . the power of his imagination. So, Coyote began to think . . .

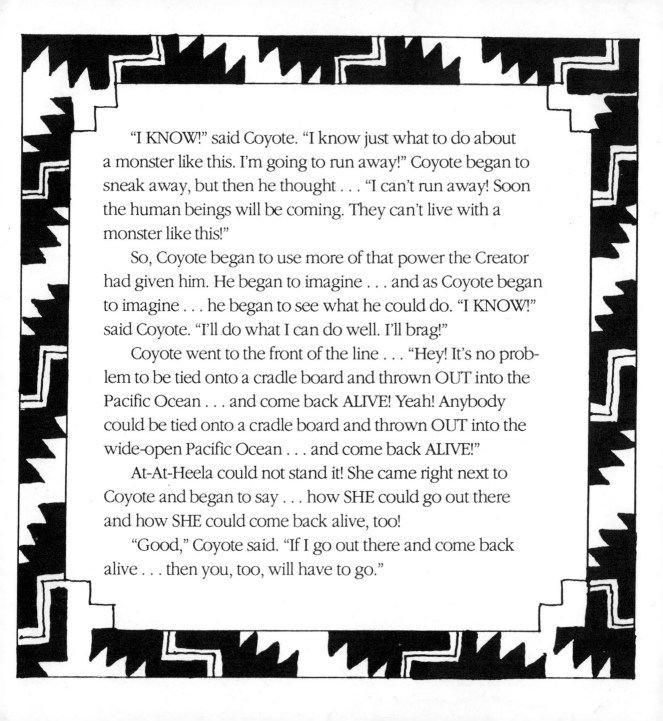

"I KNOW!" said Coyote. "I know just what to do about a monster like this. I'm going to run away!" Coyote began to sneak away, but then he thought . . . "I can't run away! Soon the human beings will be coming. They can't live with a monster like this!"

So, Coyote began to use more of that power the Creator had given him. He began to imagine . . . and as Coyote began to imagine . . . he began to see what he could do. "I KNOW!" said Coyote. "I'll do what I can do well. I'll brag!"

Coyote went to the front of the line . . . "Hey! It's no problem to be tied onto a cradle board and thrown OUT into the Pacific Ocean . . . and come back ALIVE! Yeah! Anybody could be tied onto a cradle board and thrown OUT into the wide-open Pacific Ocean . . . and come back ALIVE!"

At-At-Heela could not stand it! She came right next to Coyote and began to say . . . how SHE could go out there and how SHE could come back alive, too!

"Good," Coyote said. "If I go out there and come back alive . . . then you, too, will have to go."

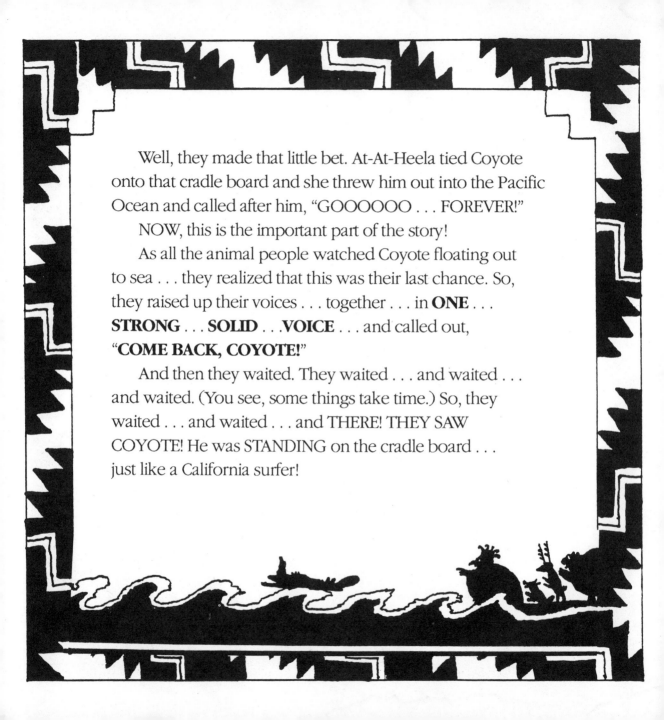

Well, they made that little bet. At-At-Heela tied Coyote onto that cradle board and she threw him out into the Pacific Ocean and called after him, "GOOOOOO . . . FOREVER!"

NOW, this is the important part of the story!

As all the animal people watched Coyote floating out to sea . . . they realized that this was their last chance. So, they raised up their voices . . . together . . . in **ONE** . . . **STRONG** . . . **SOLID** . . .**VOICE** . . . and called out, **"COME BACK, COYOTE!"**

And then they waited. They waited . . . and waited . . . and waited. (You see, some things take time.) So, they waited . . . and waited . . . and THERE! THEY SAW COYOTE! He was STANDING on the cradle board . . . just like a California surfer!

He came up onto the beach. He tied At-At-Heela onto the board and threw her OUT into the Pacific Ocean. Coyote and ALL THE ANIMAL PEOPLE called after her . . . "GOOOOOO . . . FOREVER!"

And Coyote said, "And don't bother coming back!"

And you see, that one . . . she has never come back . . . because none of our women are like her.

But still to this day, people will go to the Pacific Ocean . . . they will stare out at the ocean . . . and nobody really knows why!

Coyote said, "It is a very good thing I am doing!" And he went on his way . . . making those tracks, tracks, tracks, tracks.

Coyote and Spider Woman
Karok (Northern California)

Coyote was going on his way . . . down into a beautiful green valley in Northern California. It was there . . . that Ol' Man Coyote . . . met up with Ol' Woman Coyote. It was not very long after that, that Ol' Man Coyote and Ol' Woman Coyote were living in the very same den. And it was not very long after that, that there were two little pup Coyotes living there, too.

These pups were so cute! Every morning . . . they would come out of their den and sing! "Yip, yip, yip, yearuuuuu, yip, yip, yip, ye-ruuuuu, uuuuu!" Well . . . they were learning how to sing. Like us two-leggeds, many animal people like to sing. Coyote people are especially good singers. They start practicing when they are still very little.

One day, Ol' Woman Coyote said to Ol' Man Coyote, "Hey, I'm going out to dig some roots for tonight's supper. You stay here and watch those pups. DON'T YOU LEAVE THOSE PUPS IN THE SUN TOO LONG. IF YOU LEAVE THEM IN THE SUN, THEY WILL SURELY DIE OF HEAT STROKE." And she went off.

Now, Coyote was watching his pups . . . for a while. Soon, he began to smell some salmon that his neighbor was roasting. Coyote decided to go visit his neighbor . . . Oh, yes! Coyote did that! He was over at his neighbor's lodge eating salmon and talking and talking. When he came home . . . later that afternoon . . . there were his pups, sick on the ground.

"It is not MY FAULT," said Coyote, "that my pups are sick . . . Noooo . . . IT IS THE SUN'S FAULT! I will go up into the sky and KILL THAT SUN and TEACH HIM A LESSON!"

So, Coyote took out an arrow . . . and shot it into the sky . . . *Wwwwwwwing . . . thung!* It STUCK in the sky! He took out another . . . *Wwwwwwwing . . . thung!* This arrow stuck right into the end of the first arrow! He took another . . . *Wwwwwwwing . . . thung!* And another . . . *wwwwwwwing . . .*

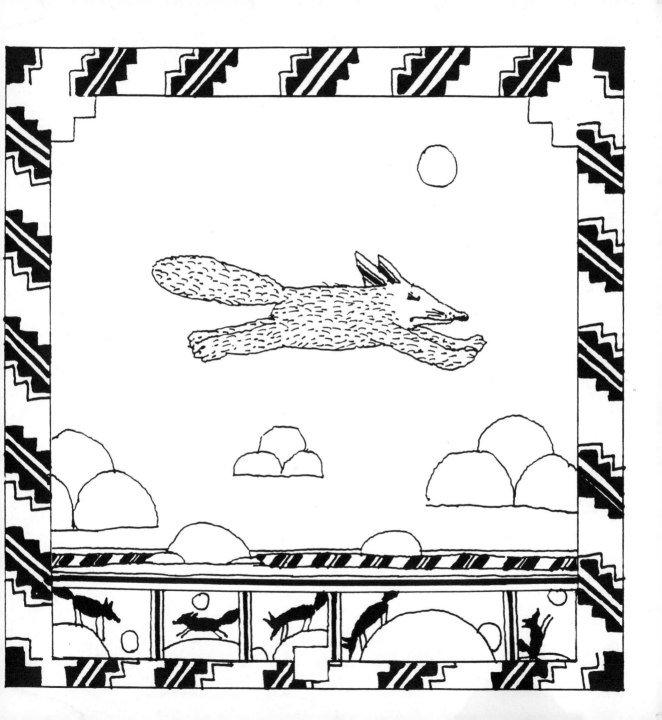

thung! . . . and another . . . until there was a long ladder of arrows coming out of the sky. Coyote climbed up this ladder . . . way up into the sky world.

When he got up into the sky world, he saw the sun . . . just going down in the west. "Good!" said Coyote. "I'll run across the sky and cut him off at the pass." So, Coyote ran to the edge of the sky. But as he got to the edge, the sun . . . *Pth-th-th-thrup!* . . . went DOWN in the WEST! "HEY!" Coyote screamed. "COME BACK AND FIGHT! YOU BIG BALL OF HOT GAS! WHAT ARE YOU, ANYWAY? A SUN . . . OR A CHICKEN?

Coyote was up there screaming insults at the sun, when all at once, the sun . . . *Pth-th-th-thrup!* . . . came UP in the EAST! "HEY!" screamed Coyote, and he ran across the sky. But as Coyote ran east the sun passed over his head going west. "Hey!" Coyote ran back to the west. But by the time he got to the edge of the sky in the west, the sun had just gone down. "HEY! YOU BALL OF HOT GAS!" Coyote was screaming insults at the sun . . .when . . . the sun peeked UP in the EAST! "HEY!"

Well . . . the animal people back on the earth were watching Coyote running this way. . . and that . . . east and west . . . up . . . and back . . . screaming insults at the sun.

Suddenly, Coyote STOPPED! . . . dead center in his sky tracks, with his tongue hanging out of his mouth. "Hh, hh, hh, hh, hmmm . . ." Coyote thought . . . "Maybe it's not such a good idea to try to kill the sun?" And anyway, he was missing Ol' Woman Coyote. So, he decided to go home . . . but, how was he going to do this?

Well, he asked for a little help . . . from Xah . . . Xah, Spider Woman. Everyone knows that Spider Woman makes the strongest rope! And she did that! She made some of her good strong rope . . . and soon Coyote was going down . . . down . . . down . . . on that rope . . . and as he was going down, he was looking up there . . . at where that rope was coming from. It was coming out of the end of Spider's butt. Well, actually, it was her abdomen, but it looked like a butt to Coyote, and so, he started giggling about it . . . as he was going down . . . "Che-he-he . . . Spider's butt . . . che-he-he." Spider woman could hear Coyote laughing! She pulled Coyote back up into the sky. "Hey, Coyote!" She was waving all eight legs at once. "I am helping you . . . and you are laughing at my butt! That is not very nice."

"Oh yes, sister, I knew I should not have laughed at your butt. I knew this, I . . . just . . . ah . . . FORGOT! Please sister, just give me one more chance. I promise, this time I won't laugh at your butt."

Well . . . Xah let Coyote down on her rope a second time.

Coyote was going down . . . down . . . down . . . on Spider's rope . . . and he was trying NOT to look at where that rope was coming from. But, after some time . . . he peeked! "Che-he-he . . . look at that big butt . . . che-he-he." Even though Coyote was only snickering, Spider Woman could hear it! She pulled him back up into the sky . . . "OK, Coyote. Now look, I am helping you . . . and you are laughing at me. That is not very nice."

"Ooooh yes," said Coyote, "Yes, yes, I knew this! I knew I shouldn't have laughed . . . I knew this . . . I just . . . FOR-GOT! PLEASE sister, let me down just one more time. I PROMISE . . . THIS TIME I will not laugh at your butt."

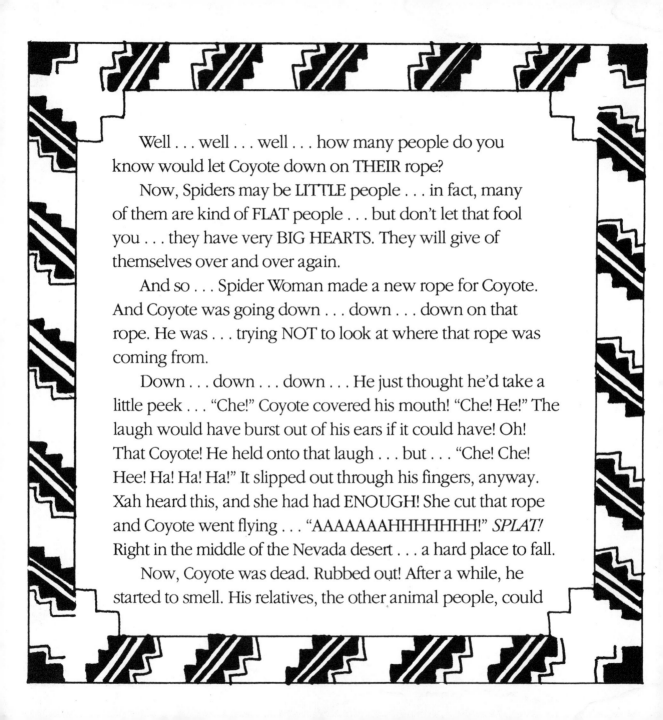

Well . . . well . . . well . . . how many people do you know would let Coyote down on THEIR rope?

Now, Spiders may be LITTLE people . . . in fact, many of them are kind of FLAT people . . . but don't let that fool you . . . they have very BIG HEARTS. They will give of themselves over and over again.

And so . . . Spider Woman made a new rope for Coyote. And Coyote was going down . . . down . . . down on that rope. He was . . . trying NOT to look at where that rope was coming from.

Down . . . down . . . down . . . He just thought he'd take a little peek . . . "Che!" Coyote covered his mouth! "Che! He!" The laugh would have burst out of his ears if it could have! Oh! That Coyote! He held onto that laugh . . . but . . . "Che! Che! Hee! Ha! Ha! Ha!" It slipped out through his fingers, anyway. Xah heard this, and she had had ENOUGH! She cut that rope and Coyote went flying . . . "AAAAAAAHHHHHHH!" *SPLAT!* Right in the middle of the Nevada desert . . . a hard place to fall.

Now, Coyote was dead. Rubbed out! After a while, he started to smell. His relatives, the other animal people, could

smell Coyote. They came to that place . . . "Hey look! Coyote's dead! Good! Let's eat him up." They started to eat Coyote. They ate all his meat. They ate out his insides. They ate his eyeballs. They ate up everything . . . except for his bones.

Then . . . these little insect people came and ate little holes in those bones . . . and then . . . that . . . *woooooh* . . . wind came by . . . and those bones began to sing . . . "COYYYYOOOOOOOOOOTEEEEEEE" . . .

Now, Fox, Coyote's younger brother, heard those bones singing . . . he heard those bones singing off somewhere . . . so, he followed their song until he came upon those singing bones and said, "Yip! Yip! Coyote has been fooling around again!"

So, Fox jumped over those bones. He jumped over Coyote's bones four times . . . four times for each of the four directions . . . and on the fourth time, those bones came . . . *Pth-th-thrup!* . . . BACK TO LIFE! . . . as Ol' Man Coyote.

"Aaaawh!" yawned Coyote, "I have had a long sleep." Then, he went right on his way again . . . making those tracks, tracks . . . tracks, tracks, tracks.

Coyote and the Grass People
Assiniboin (Great Plains)

Tracks, tracks, tracks . . . That day, Coyote was loping along in the wide-open grasslands of the Great Plains. He was feeling big about himself that day. He had brought the salmon to the Columbia River. He had killed a great monster. So, he was feeling especially big about himself that day. He started to feel SO BIG about himself that he started bragging: "It is a very good thing I am doing. Soon the two-leggeds will be coming."

All of a sudden . . . he heard it! That song! Someone was singing off somewhere . . . softly . . . "Wwwww . . . we are the strongest people in the world."

"Who is singing that?" asked Coyote. He looked around. No one was there.

He went on . . . tracks, tracks . . .

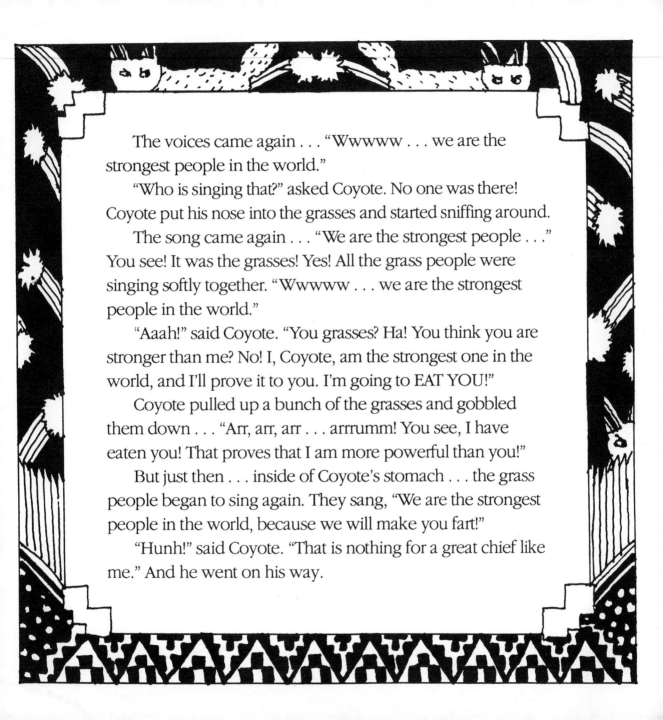

The voices came again . . . "Wwwww . . . we are the strongest people in the world."

"Who is singing that?" asked Coyote. No one was there! Coyote put his nose into the grasses and started sniffing around.

The song came again . . . "We are the strongest people . . ." You see! It was the grasses! Yes! All the grass people were singing softly together. "Wwwww . . . we are the strongest people in the world."

"Aaah!" said Coyote. "You grasses? Ha! You think you are stronger than me? No! I, Coyote, am the strongest one in the world, and I'll prove it to you. I'm going to EAT YOU!"

Coyote pulled up a bunch of the grasses and gobbled them down . . . "Arr, arr, arr . . . arrrumm! You see, I have eaten you! That proves that I am more powerful than you!"

But just then . . . inside of Coyote's stomach . . . the grass people began to sing again. They sang, "We are the strongest people in the world, because we will make you fart!"

"Hunh!" said Coyote. "That is nothing for a great chief like me." And he went on his way.

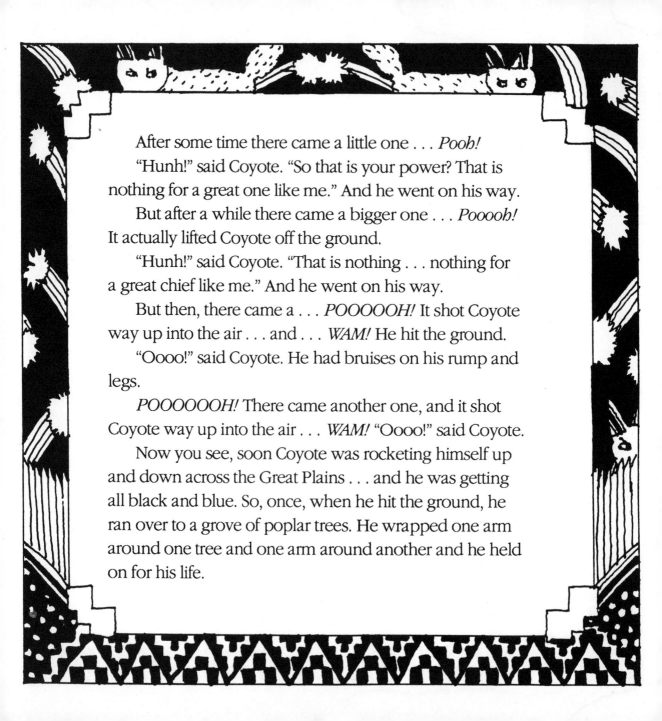

After some time there came a little one . . . *Pooh!*

"Hunh!" said Coyote. "So that is your power? That is nothing for a great one like me." And he went on his way.

But after a while there came a bigger one . . . *Poooob!* It actually lifted Coyote off the ground.

"Hunh!" said Coyote. "That is nothing . . . nothing for a great chief like me." And he went on his way.

But then, there came a . . . *POOOOOH!* It shot Coyote way up into the air . . . and . . . *WAM!* He hit the ground.

"Oooo!" said Coyote. He had bruises on his rump and legs.

POOOOOOH! There came another one, and it shot Coyote way up into the air . . . *WAM!* "Oooo!" said Coyote.

Now you see, soon Coyote was rocketing himself up and down across the Great Plains . . . and he was getting all black and blue. So, once, when he hit the ground, he ran over to a grove of poplar trees. He wrapped one arm around one tree and one arm around another and he held on for his life.

There he was . . . *"POOOH! POOOH! POOOH!"* . . . exploding away.

As he fired away the trees started to pull loose from the earth . . . *Eeh . . . eeeh . . . eeeeeeeeh . . .* But luckily, it finally stopped . . . and Coyote went on his way.

But, if you look at poplar trees today, you will see . . . they look as if someone tried to pull them out of the ground. They look like that because Old Man Coyote was there, passing on the grass people's power.

Tracks, tracks . . . tracks, tracks, tracks . . .

Railroad Coyote

That coyote could be seen ramblin' along the railroad tracks most weekdays about one o'clock in the afternoon. It was a little after one that the train bound for Nevada swept through the valley. That coyote drifted about from side to side as much as he was progressing forward. Coyote kept his nose to the ground as if there were something of interest on that side of the tracks.

On the other side of the tracks, ground squirrels had taken cover in their tunnels under the earth. Far up the tracks, other ground squirrels sat up, out of their holes watching coyote.

When the train came storming by, coyote picked up his gait to a full, shotgun gallop. He raced that train until the last car passed . . . opening the tracks to his view again. He leaped directly over the tracks. . . much to the surprise of the ground squirrels . . . and caught one in his mouth. That railroad coyote trick worked again!

"Just who is Coyote? Is he a man . . . or an animal . . . or a spirit?"

Kindergarten student

AUDIO TAPES FROM
SUSAN STRAUSS
STORYTELLER

Coyote Gets A Cadillac
& Other Eye Opening Earth Tales $10

Tracks, Tracks, Tracks (Coyote Tales) $10

And For Kids (ages 6 & up) $10

Witches, Queens & Goddesses:
Mythological Images of the Feminine $10

The Bird's Tale: World Bird Myths $10

Yiddish & Hassidic Tales $10

Add postage: $2.50 for 1-2 items, $3.50 or 3 or more

Order from:
SUSAN STRAUSS
P.O. Box 1141
Bend, OR 97709
Phone: 503-382-2888

Beyond Words Publishing
Toll free 800-284-9673

Acknowledgments

Susan Strauss would like to gratefully acknowledge the following people: Leslie Spier, whose article "The Sinkaietk or Southern Okanagon of Washington," provided the inspiration for "Coyote Gets His Power," Edward S. Curtis, whose story "Coyote at the Mouth of the Columbia River," is the basis for "Monster Woman at the Coast," William Bright and Gladys Nomland, whose research at the University of California supplied the heart for "Coyote and Spider Woman," and Robert Lowie, whose book *The Assiniboin,* led to "Coyote and the Grass People."